# ODIN'S MONSTER

**Susan Price**

**Illustrated by Patrick Lynch**

**A & C Black · London**

**The Comets Series**

Series Editor, Amy Gibbs

| | |
|---|---|
| **King Fernando** | John Bartholomew |
| **A Witch in Time** | Terry Deary |
| **Tom's Sausage Lion** | Michael Morpurgo |
| **Odin's Monster** | Susan Price |
| **The Air-Raid Shelter** | Jeremy Strong |

Price, Susan
    Odin's monster.—(Comets)
    I. Title    II. Price, Alison
    823'.914[J]    PZ7
    ISBN 0-7136-2787-5

Published by A & C Black (Publishers) Limited
35 Bedford Row, London WC1R 4JH

Text © 1986 Susan Price
Illustrations © 1986 Patrick Lynch
First published 1986

ISBN 0-7136-2787-5

Filmset by August Filmsetting, Haydock, St Helens
Printed in Great Britain by R J Acford Ltd., Chichester

## Odin's Monster

Odin was the god of Death, of poetry and dangerous magic. Thor was the god who guarded homes and families. Freya, the Lady, and her brother Frey, were the twin gods who made the corn grow, the sheep to have lambs, and men and women to have children. A thousand years ago, the people of Iceland prayed to them all.

Odin was the witches' god. When they asked for His help, He lent them His power. He taught them the spell of the goatskins, by which they could raise thick fogs so travellers lost their way, and ships wrecked and sailors drowned. He gave them witch-sight, making them able to kill people with one angry look from their eyes, or blight a field so nothing would grow there, and the farmers went hungry. This power of the witches was strongest in the dark, so they were at their worst in winter – for during the winter, in Iceland, daylight never comes. From winter's beginning to winter's end, all is darkness and witch-work.

There was a man named Kveldulf Egillsson, who was always called Kveldulf Witch. He worshipped Odin. He was a big, grey-bearded man with a head of thick, uncombed grey hair, so long that he tucked it under his belt. He had fought in battles in Ireland, Scotland, England and Russia; and he was not a pleasant man to have dealings with. He did not keep his promises, and would cheat anyone if he could.

Kveldulf lived alone on his farm. No one visited him. People stayed as far from his house as they could, especially after dark. 'Kveldulf' means 'Evening Wolf', and it was said that Kveldulf changed his shape when evening came. But whether that's true or not, who knows?

Kveldulf kept a raven. It was no ordinary raven, but a bird he had killed and brought back to life by giving it a human soul, with Odin's help. The raven, with its human soul, was able to talk and to understand human speech. It flew about everywhere, near and far, spying on people and bringing all the news back to Kveldulf.

When Odin helped a man to do such magic as that, Odin had to be paid; and Odin was always paid with a man's life. To thank Odin for his raven, Kveldulf killed a man. Kveldulf had killed many men, and had never been punished. People were too afraid of him.

Kveldulf's raven was once away for weeks. When it returned, it flew to his chair-back and said, 'I have been to Ultima Thule, Kveldulf!'

Ultima Thule was a land still further north than Iceland, on the very top and edge of the world.

'And what did you see there, bird?' Kveldulf asked.

'I saw the Queen of Ultima Thule in her palace. I flew close and heard what her advisers were telling her. They were saying, "It's time you married, Queen. You must have a daughter to rule after you are dead."'

'And what did the Queen say to that?' asked Kveldulf Witch.

'She said, "I am a witch, a warrior and a Queen. No ordinary marriage will do for me." So I flew home to bring you this news.' And the raven knocked its big beak on the wooden chair.

Kveldulf became thoughtful. What kind of husband would be sought by a Queen who was also a witch and a warrior? Why, thought Kveldulf, she would want a husband who was also a warrior and a witch: an even more skilful witch and a greater warrior than she was herself. And I, thought Kveldulf, I am a warrior and a witch.

He thought of himself as King of Ultima Thule.

Kveldulf wondered how to make himself pleasing to the Queen of Ultima Thule. 'Raven!' he said. 'Tell me, who is the best word-user in Iceland?'

The raven said, 'Thord Cat is.'

'How good is he?' asked the witch.

'Thord Cat can tell a story about water leaking from a bucket, and keep everyone listening all night.'

Kveldulf nodded. 'He is the man I need. I shall take him with me to Ultima Thule, and I shall have him tell the story of my life to the Queen. His words will be so clever, and so full of praise for me, that they will make the Queen fall in love with me. Tell me more about him, bird.'

'He is well liked by people,' said the raven, 'because he is handsome and polite. His favourite god is The Lady, Freya. He farms at Thrainsstead with his brothers, Haki and Grimm.'

'Thrainsstead? That's Thrain Thorsson's farm,' Kveldulf said.

6

'Thrain Thorsson died years ago, and his wife died before him,' said the raven. 'Haki, Grimm and Thord are their sons.'

'In the old days, Thrain Thorsson was a friend to me,' Kveldulf said. 'His son should be pleased to make a speech in my honour.'

So Kveldulf saddled his horse and rode over to Thrainsstead. On his way he met an old beggar-woman who was trudging along the hillside tracks. She was all rags and bones, and her back was so bent that her head was always looking down. Yet for all her age she was getting along at a good speed.

Kveldulf was not interested in her, and would have ridden past without speaking, except that she stepped in front of his horse.

'Master! I am trying to find Thrainsstead. Can you tell me where it is?'

Kveldulf was angry at having to rein in his horse. 'Why do you want to go there?'

'I've heard that the people are kind and would let me stay there for the winter,' the old woman answered.

'Well, I'm going to Thrainsstead,' said Kveldulf. 'Follow me!' And he kicked up his horse and rode past her, laughing because he thought the old woman could not keep up with him.

He didn't look back, and so didn't see the old woman leave the path, bound up the side of a rough, steep slope, and disappear over the top.

Kveldulf rode on and reached Thrainsstead, a long farmhouse built of grass-grown turfs and looking like a grassy hillock. Around it were other hillocks, of different sizes, which were really store-houses, sheep-sheds and cow-byres.

It was the time of year when the sheep were gathered in from the mountainsides, and the cattle from the hill-meadows, so none of the Thrainsson brothers were at home. But Kveldulf spoke to the women who were working about the place, and bands of children were sent to the hillsides, to find Thord Cat and bring him home.

Kveldulf went into the farmhouse and sat himself down in the guest-chair by the fire. Two decorated wooden pillars stood on either side of the chair; and on the other side of the house was another big chair between two more wooden pillars. On the wall behind the guest-chair was a silver Thor's Hammer, the sign of Thor, hung there to keep the house safe.

Along the middle of the house's floor, from end to end, ran a stone-paved trench, where fires were built. On very cold days, it held a long-fire, burning from one end of the house to the other.

Kveldulf had sat a long while before there came in a big, blond man, so tall that he had to duck to keep his head from bumping the rafters. But this man wasn't Thord Cat. This was Haki Thrainsson, the eldest of the brothers. The children had told him about the visitor and he had come down from the mountain to see who it was. He was not pleased to discover that it was Kveldulf Witch, but he was polite, and sat, and talked.

In came another, even taller, broader man. This wasn't Thord Cat either. This was Grimm Thrainsson, and he too had come to see who their visitor was. He was no better pleased to see the witch in their guest-seat, but he didn't show it.

The next person to come in surprised Kveldulf, for it was the old beggar-woman he had passed on his way. How had she, without a horse, reached the farm as soon as this? Kveldulf couldn't understand it, and it annoyed him.

Behind the old woman came Thord Cat, and at the sight of him, Kveldulf was shocked. He had expected Thord to be a big man, like Haki and Grimm; but instead Thord Cat was small, half the size of his brothers, and young too. A little scrap of a man, with a small head, small hands, small feet. A ginger cat was riding on Thord's shoulder, and purring as it rubbed its small, neat round head against Thord's. Thord's hair was redder than the cat's fur. The ginger cat and Thord Cat both looked at Kveldulf with the same large-eyed, still, solemn stare. This stare also annoyed Kveldulf.

Thord Cat nodded politely to Kveldulf, but

spoke to his eldest brother. 'Haki,' he said, 'this is Bergthora, and she will be on the roads this winter unless she can stay with us. I said she could.'

'You're welcome here,' said Haki to the old beggar-woman, Bergthora.

Thord Cat then looked at Kveldulf again, and Kveldulf looked at him. It was easy to see that they didn't like each other. Thord sat on the floor with his feet in the fire-trench, and the cat came down from his shoulder into his lap.

'I've heard you are the best story-teller in Iceland, Thord Cat,' Kveldulf said, 'but when I look at you, I find it hard to believe.'

'The Kings of Norway, Denmark and England haven't a better story-teller than Our Cat,' said Grimm.

'I want a story making about *me*,' said Kveldulf. 'I want the story of my life told.'

Haki and Grimm would have laughed, except that it wasn't wise to laugh at Kveldulf Witch.

Kveldulf asked, 'Do you think you could tell my story, Short-Stuff?'

'I think I could,' said Thord Cat. The cat in his lap neatly and politely cleaned its face. Bergthora served herself from a pot of porridge by the fire, and sat eating it and listening.

'It won't be difficult because I'll tell you what to say,' Kveldulf told Thord. 'You must put in something about all the countries I've sailed to – and a lot about all the battles I've fought in and all the people I've killed. Say I'm a mighty warrior! Put in that I'm a good-looking man for my age. I'm not as pretty as you with your red hair, but you must say that a wise old man who's seen everything is worth more than a young one who knows nothing. Have you got all that, Knee-High?'

'Oh, yes,' said Thord Cat.

'Good. You're doing well. Say that I'm rich – and that I'm a skilful witch. But don't say it like I've said it here. Stretch it all out and dress it up in fancy words, the way you story-tellers do. Can you manage that, Dwarf?'

'Yes,' Thord Cat said.

'Good,' said Kveldulf.

'But I won't,' said Thord, and he and the ginger cat looked up at the witch in a way that made Kveldulf furious.

'We are honest people here,' Thord Cat said. 'You are a killer, a promise-breaker and a witch. We don't deal with people like you.'

Haki and Grimm shifted nervously at these words of Thord's, as if they wished he had not spoken them.

'Wherever I go, people speak to me with respect, Thord Cat,' Kveldulf said.

'When our father was still alive,' said Thord, 'you came here, begging for hay to feed your cow through the winter. We hadn't much hay to feed our own animals, but our father gave you the hay you wanted.'

'Your father was a friend to me, and he would have advised you to be a friend to me also,' said Kveldulf.

'Two years later,' Thord went on, 'we had a bad harvest, and my father was forced to beg for hay. *You* had more than you needed, Kveldulf, but you wouldn't give our father any, even though he had helped you. So our sheep died, and our mother died too, that year. And you come asking *me* to tell your story! You Odin-worshippers are all alike. Your god is a promise-breaker and a killer, and you worship Him by killing and breaking promises yourselves.'

Quietly, Kveldulf said, 'I hear that you worship Freya, little Thord Cat. A small god for a small man!'

'I owe Freya my special worship,' Thord said.

Haki spoke up. 'When Thord was born, our mother thought he would die, he was so small and ill.'

'So our mother prayed to The Lady Freya,' said Grimm.

'And that night, as our mother was lying awake – ' said Haki.

' – She smelt a fine smell, like a breeze blowing through a field of grass and flowers,' said Thord Cat, 'and it grew much lighter, as if all the lamps had suddenly been lit.'

'And our mother looked and saw Freya. Freya had come into the house,' said Grimm.

'Freya picked our Thord up from his cradle,' said Haki.

Thord said, 'Because I was ill, She wept.'

'Her tears fell on his face,' said Haki.

'And Freya's tears are liquid gold,' said Thord.

'She laid him down and went away,' said Haki, 'and he's never been ill since, never in his life.'

'And his hair was red, when it grew,' said Grimm.

'So, we have a special love for Freya in this house,' said Haki.

Thord looked at Kveldulf and said, 'It's because Freya's tears fell on me that I have a knack for words; and I won't use the gift She gave me to make praise of a man like you. There are plenty of other story-tellers in Iceland. See if one of them will tell your story for you.'

The more Thord refused to tell the story, the more Kveldulf wanted him to tell it. That was the way Kveldulf was.

Kveldulf said, 'Thord Kitten, it will be better for you and your brothers if you do as I ask.'

Because Thord was such a little man, he was always careful to behave bravely, so people could never say, 'Thord is afraid of everything and everyone because he is little and weak.'

'It's best for my brothers and me if we have nothing to do with you, Kveldulf Witch,' he said.

'You don't know the power I have, Thord Kitten,' said Kveldulf. 'I can do more than blight fields. If you will not tell my story, I shall make a Sending and set it against you.'

'We are not afraid of your threats,' Thord said. 'Freya will protect us.'

Kveldulf said no more, but left the house. Anyone could see that he was angry.

After he had gone, Bergthora said, 'A Sending is a monster.'

Haki said, 'You spoke up to the witch bravely, Cat. Let's hope that Freya does protect us.'

Then the brothers went back to their work.

Kveldulf rode home to his farm in an evil temper. He would not have cared so much if Thord Cat had been older, or a bigger man – but to be called a killer and a cheat, and to be turned away by someone whose head hardly reached his shoulder was more than he could stand.

'I will have my story told by Thord Cat, and I

will see Thord Cat dead,' Kveldulf swore. 'Odin! Help me in this! Lend me Your power, let me force Thord Cat to obey me, and I promise that once his words have made me King of Ultima Thule, I will give You his life in payment.' And, as he said this, Kveldulf felt that the power of his terrible god was with him.

Kveldulf made a Sending. It took him a long time. By the time it was made, winter had come. Every day was shorter, colder, darker. Every hour of darkness made Kveldulf's witch-power stronger. Just after the first snows had fallen, he sent the Sending against the Thrainssons.

In winter, when daylight was so scarce, the people left the house only to feed and water the animals in the sheds, or to visit the privy themselves. Haki went out to the sheep-sheds one morning, just after breakfast. He came back sooner than expected, with a face as white as snow, and shaking so hard he could scarcely walk or stand. They sat him down, and begged him to tell them what had happened.

'A something came walking across the yard towards me,' Haki said. 'Its skin hung in rags and dragged behind it. And worse, worse! It *spoke* to me!'

'What did it say?' old Bergthora asked.

'The way its mouth moved was horrible,' said

Haki. 'It said to me, "Go to your brother, Thord Kitten, and tell him that if he never wants to see me himself, he must tell Kveldulf's story." Then it went away – but it had come so close that its skin dragged over my foot!'

Bergthora grabbed Thord by the arm and said, 'It is Kveldulf's Sending!'

No one wanted to go outside. They were all terrified of meeting whatever it had been that Haki had met. To show how unafraid he was, Thord went out by himself to feed the animals, not even bothering to turn his head to see where the Sending might be. Thord was as much afraid as everyone else, and his legs shook when he stood still; but he was determined not to let anyone see his fear. After a day of watching Thord go out into the dark by himself, the others at Thrainsstead were ashamed, and began doing their share of the work again – but they were constantly looking behind them, and peering into dark corners; and they went about in groups of two or three.

But days went by and no one saw anything alarming; and they began to joke about what Haki had seen – until Grimm went out to the privy one dark afternoon. He was coming back across the yard when he heard a woman's voice call his name. He stopped and peered about in the gloom, but could see no one near him. The voice came again, and seemed to come from the house-roof. On the roof, over the doorway, lay the Sending.

Grimm's heart beat on his ribs as the clapper of a bell beats on a bell's sides. He dared not try to go into the house while the Sending lay above the door.

Grimm was still standing there, in the dark and cold, when Haki came to the door. 'Grimm! Why are you standing there? Come in!' Haki said.

Grimm raised his arm and pointed to the roof above Haki's head.

Haki was inside the house and could not see what Grimm was pointing at, but he guessed, and was afraid to go out. He shouted, and others came running to the door. But when Thord reached the door there was a loud noise from the roof, like the noise made by the sheep and cattle when they climbed on the roof to eat the grass growing there. A dragging sound followed, as if a heavy piece of leather was being dragged over the roof. The noise faded away.

'It's gone,' Grimm called to them from the yard.

Thord and Haki helped their brother into the house. They sat him by the fire, gave him hot stew, and asked him what he had seen.

'It was Kveldulf's Sending. It could have been nothing else,' he said. 'It lay on the roof and looked at me. It has eyes like boiled eggs with the shells off. It has no eyelids, Cat, and can't close them. No skin and no eyelids.'

'How could you see it so well in this dark?' Haki asked.

'It had lights burning on its horns!'

'Did it say anything to you?' asked old Bergthora.

Grimm looked round for Thord and fixed his gaze on him. 'The thing said to me, "Tell your brother Thord that if he doesn't tell Kveldulf's story, I shall visit *him* in three day's time. Doors and locks won't keep me out. Tell Thord that."'

Everyone in the household stared at Thord then, and Thord blushed with annoyance. 'You think I should give in just because Kveldulf sends this monster against us,' he said. 'But that would be a cowardly thing to do.' And he went away into a corner by himself where he hoped no one would bother him.

Haki and Grimm looked at each other. 'When he sees the Sending himself, he will tell the story,' said Haki.

'I think we should leave here,' said Grimm, who was still shaking from his fright and cold. 'I don't care how bad the weather is, we should go to our aunt, Unn. She will take us in.'

'What would be the good of that?' asked old Bergthora. 'Kveldulf would send his monster to wherever Thord was. Do you want your aunt to be plagued with it?'

Grimm and Haki looked over at Thord, who was sitting hunched in a corner. They were both thinking that they could go to their aunt and leave Thord behind at Thrainsstead. Then the Sending would only torment Thord.

'Whatever happens, we must all stick together, and defend each other,' said Haki, and Grimm agreed. So they stayed at Thrainsstead.

Two days passed. The people went about the business of life without ever mentioning the Sending. Thord was unusually quiet.

On the third day the Sending was in everyone's thoughts. Everyone was wondering when it would come, but still no one spoke of it.

There was no way of telling when night came, for the afternoon had been as dark as night. But the people wanted to behave normally. One by one the household laid themselves down on the floor to go to sleep.

Not many of them slept. They lay awake, waiting.

The light of the fire made everything in the long, low house a dark red or a most lightless black. No one spoke or even snored. Sometimes the sound of the fire burning in the silence was like small, quiet footsteps approaching, or something dragging.

Thord Cat lay on his back, pretending to be asleep. He was dozing when he felt Haki or Grimm lean on him. One of them was leaning an elbow on his chest, pressing down on his ribs. It hurt, and the weight became heavier, and heavier.

Thord opened his eyes. Staring into his own were two great, round white eyes, bulging like shelled boiled eggs, and shining in the firelight.

The eyes were sticking out of a big head. Higher than the eyes were two long horns, shining sharp.

The Sending had come, and it was lying on top of him.

It lay there, heavier and heavier. Thord found it hard to breathe. He thought his ribs would soon be snapped and pressed flat. He wriggled and struggled to get from beneath the Sending, but could not move an arm or a leg; and the struggling made him so breathless that he began to choke for lack of air and could not call to his brothers for help. The Sending was suffocating him. And all the time it stared into his face with its bulging, lidless eyes.

And the monster spoke to him in the thin little voice of a small girl. It said, 'Now, Thord Kitten, listen to me. Do you see my horns?' It wagged its head. 'I shall use these horns to cut you into slices unless you tell Kveldulf's story. Do you feel my hooves? They are cloven and as sharp as knife-blades. I will trample you into a mash with them unless you tell the story.'

Thord gathered together all the breath he could, and gasped, 'If – you don't – let me breathe – I won't be able to – tell stories.'

The Sending understood that it was doing its job too well, and killing the story-teller before he had told the story. It heaved itself up to take its weight from Thord's chest.

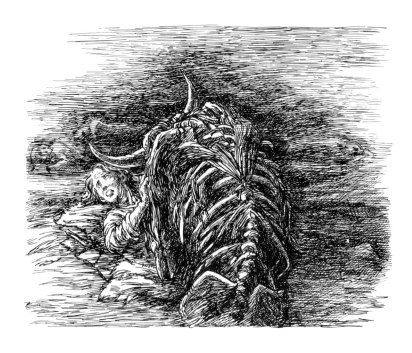

Thord took three good breaths, and yelled, 'Freya! Help me!'

The Sending roared, and rose in the air. Thord rolled away and into the fire-trench. He lay at the trench bottom, trying to get his breath, his ears filled with the roaring and trampling of the Sending. All about, people were waking and crying out in surprise and fright, shrieking at the sight of the huge shadow that rushed along the walls and ceiling. Haki and Grimm were yelling for Thord; the Sending thrashed its dangling skin; and Thord, whenever he had the breath, shouted, 'Freya protect us!'

Bergthora was scrambling about in the dark, lighting the oil-lamps at the fire. More and more she lit, and their light flared up, yellow and smoky. The more light there was, the less the noise seemed and the quieter people became. Bergthora took a lamp to where Thord was lying in the fire-trench, hiding his head.

'Ssh,' she said. 'Freya has answered you. The Sending has gone.'

Haki stirred the fire and it burned up and melted away more of the shadows. Thord looked down the long length of the house. He saw wild faces, but they were all the familiar faces of people woken suddenly from a doze. There were no monsters. A comforting smell of wood and oil smoke filled his nose.

Haki and Grimm came up. 'Now you've seen it

for yourself, are you going to do as Kveldulf asks?' Grimm said.

'Freya protected me,' Thord said.

'She didn't do much to protect Haki and me,' said Grimm.

'We must not let this witch and his promise-breaking god bully us,' Thord said.

The Sending flew home to its maker and master, Kveldulf. He knew it was coming and opened his door to let it in. 'Well?' he said, as the Sending dragged its trailing skin into his house.

'I did as you ordered,' the Sending told him. 'I thought he would agree to tell your story – but instead he called for Freya, and I came away.'

'You are a creature of the most powerful of the gods – Odin!' Kveldulf yelled. 'You have no need to fear Freya, fool! Go back and lie on him again!'

The Sending grumbled. 'Don't shout at me! I fear Freya when I'm in that house. Those brothers never praise Odin, but they are thanking and praising Freya every day! When the little story-teller called for Freya, She stepped so close, I had to fly! I won't go back there tonight.'

'You will!' said Kveldulf, and he took up his witch's staff, meaning to beat the Sending with it. But the Sending lowered its head and showed him its horns, saying, 'Touch me once with that stick, old man, and I shall lie on *you*! Lift that stick to me once, and it'll be the last time you ever lift your arm.'

This is the danger of making Sendings. Once made, they are not easily controlled. Kveldulf lowered his staff.

'I have thought about it, and I have a better idea,' he said. 'No, you need not go back to Thrains-stead tonight, not now I have thought about it. Go back tomorrow instead, and drive away all the farm-people. All the women and children, all the sheep-men and cattle-men. Drive away Haki and Grimm, too. When they're all gone, and our Thord Kitten is alone with you, monster, then we'll see how brave he is, and how much faith he has in Freya.'

With that order, the haunting of Thrainsstead began.

Night and day, day and night – the one as dark as the other – the Sending came to Thrainsstead. It was afraid that Thord Cat would call for Freya, and it left him alone. No one else knew when the thing might spring out on them.

The children, when they went out to the privy, or to fetch water from the stream, would see the figure of a little girl standing just so far from them that the outlines of it melted in the dusk. They would think the figure one of themselves until they went close to it.

The men and women, going to the privy, or to the cattle and sheep, would see the figure of a man or woman, half-hidden in the shadows of a dark corner, or seeming to wait for them in the dusk outside. They would think it a friend and go to meet it.

But when approached, these dimly seen figures changed: became huge, goggling-eyed, skinless, horrible.

At other times the Sending appeared as a bear, prowling in the yard so none dared leave the house, scratching and snuffling at the door, clawing the walls.

At night it came and trampled on the roof above their heads, roaring, keeping them awake, and putting them in sweats of fear.

At breakfast it would come among them in one of its human shapes, and sit at the table. They soon learned to recognise it, whether it came as a woman, a man or a little girl, and they would sit silent, with no appetite for food, staring at the Sending in dread until it vanished.

Then, to show how much it was to be feared, it caught the head cattle-man as he crossed the yard, knocked him down and trampled him, leaving him nearly dead. After that, the more timid of the Thrainsstead people left, and went to beg for homes or shelter at other farms, which were not haunted. They left even though it was winter, and the tracks deep in snow. That was how afraid they were.

Those remaining were thin, anxious, sleepless. Thord Cat came and went about his work and his meals without speaking. Hardly anyone spoke to him. They were all thinking that he could rid them of the monster with a few words if only he would swallow his pride and agree to tell Kveldulf's story. Even Haki and Grimm were thinking this, though they would not have said so to anyone.

But Thord knew what they were thinking without being told.

Now that half the people of Thrainsstead had gone, the Sending came into the house every night, terrifying the people as it passed among them. Always it sought out either Haki or Grimm, and lay down on them, smothering them as it had once smothered Thord. Their outcries would wake everyone, but nothing could be done to drive the Sending away. It had grown bold, and laughed at the mention of Freya's name. 'I am Odin's creature!' it declared.

Once, as the thing lay on Grimm, Thord fetched an axe and chopped at it as if it was firewood. The axe sank into its sides, but did it no harm. It lay on Grimm, crushing him, and bulged its eyes at Thord, sniggering at his efforts.

'Chop until you drop, Kitten!' it said. 'You can't hurt me because I'm already dead.'

Thord was in such despair that he sat down beside Grimm and wept. The Sending laughed unkindly at his tears, and continued to jeer and laugh until Kveldulf called it home, hours later. Then it flew away, its skin flapping in the wind.

Seeing the Sending laugh at Thord's axe-blows was too much to bear for the people at Thrainsstead, and they left also. The only people remaining on the haunted farm were Haki and Grimm, Thord Cat, and old Bergthora.

Thord found that his brothers were always looking at him.

'Cat – ' Haki began.

'I won't,' Thord said.

'Cat – ' began Grimm.

'No!' said Thord. 'No!'

His brothers sighed and shook their heads.

The Sending did not bother them that night, or the next night, but on the following day Haki and Grimm went out together to feed the sheep. It was as dark as night, but they saw the Sending easily because of the lights on its horns. It was lying on the roof of the sheep-shed. It called out to them in a woman's voice. 'You have a lot of work to do now all your helpers have run away. I feel sorry for you.'

'We don't want your sympathy!' Haki said.

'I have done something helpful for you, to make your work less,' said the Sending. 'I have killed all your sheep.'

When Haki and Grimm heard this they rushed into the sheep-shed, even though the Sending lay above the door. They found it true. All of the sheep were dead. They heard the Sending's laughter going away from them through the air.

Bitterly angry, sad, and fearful, they returned to the house. They took Thord and made him sit at a table. Standing over him, they told him what the Sending had done.

'Now you see what your stubbornness has cost us,' Grimm said. 'What shall we do when spring comes – if the monster allows us to live 'til then?'

'Next it will kill our cows,' Haki said.

'Next year we shall have no milk, no butter, no meat, no wool – and no new lambs or calves. Thord, we shall starve.'

Haki put his big hand on Thord's head and covered it like a cap. 'Cat,' he said, 'we cannot afford this contest. You *must* tell Kveldulf's story.'

Old Bergthora had come close; and she was listening with interest.

Thord didn't give his brothers any answer for a long time. He didn't want to displease them, and he was trying hard to make himself believe that giving in to Kveldulf was the best thing to do.

But the more seriously he thought about making praise of Kveldulf, the sicker he felt.

He looked up at his brothers. 'Don't let us quarrel about this, please, but I won't and can't.'

Haki sat beside Thord and took his hand. 'Cat, if your enemy was a man who could be fought, we would fight with you and for you, no matter what, because you are our brother, and the youngest of us too. But we cannot fight Kveldulf. We cannot fight the Sending. If this goes on, Cat, we shall be left with nothing. It would be better if the monster killed us outright instead of chasing off our helpers and killing our animals and leaving us to starve or beg! Cat, please – your brothers beg you – make the witch his story, and save your brothers from beggary.'

'Will you, Cat?' Grimm asked.

Bergthora listened.

'I wish I *had* died when I was a baby!' Thord said.

'Give us an answer!' said Haki.

'Brothers, we mustn't quarrel,' Thord said. 'If anything at all could persuade me to praise Kveldulf, it would be your asking, Haki. But I can't give in now.'

Haki stood, and said, 'If that's your answer, Thord, then I am going to leave you to your contest with Kveldulf. I shall go to the Knoll and stay with our aunt.'

'I shall come with you,' said Grimm. 'We shall die if we stay here. You come too, Bergthora.'

They left the table to collect the things they would take with them.

Bergthora called after them, 'Aren't you ashamed to leave your young brother here alone to face the monster?'

'Don't talk nonsense, you old fool,' said Haki. 'You know as well as we do that we couldn't protect him from it if we stayed. But he can save himself at any time, with a few words.'

When Haki and Grimm were ready to begin their cold, hard, dangerous journey, they saw that old Bergthora was still sitting beside Thord.

'Aren't you coming?' Haki asked her.

'I am not! I came here to be warm through the winter, and here I'm staying, Sending or no Sending!'

'As you please,' said Haki, and he and Grimm left without another word. The cold wind blew into the house before they fastened the door after them. It was a cold leaving.

But as they trudged away, both Haki and Grimm were praying to all the gods that Thord might be kept safe, somehow.

And, inside the house, Thord was asking Freya to guard his brothers from being lost and frozen in the snow.

Without his brothers, Thord Cat felt smaller and weaker and more lonely and afraid than he had ever done in his life. He was grateful for old Bergthora's company, but dreaded the next coming of the Sending.

'Haki was right,' he said to Bergthora. 'When the Sending comes, I shall promise to tell

Kveldulf's story, however much I hate to do it.'

'Not if you've any sense,' said Bergthora. 'Oh, Kveldulf would call off the Sending. But what do you think would happen once you'd told his story, eh? With whose life do you think Kveldulf would pay his debt to Odin?'

'Mine,' said Thord. 'No matter what I do, I die.'

Bergthora slapped him on the knee and said, 'Have faith in Freya! Don't give up hope until all hope is gone!'

'You're right,' Thord said. 'Even if the monster does kill me, perhaps people will say, "Thord Cat was a little man; but he was as brave as he was small." '

'That's the way to think,' said Bergthora.

Thord didn't go to bed that night. He was sure the Sending would come, and he didn't want to be sat on.

At midnight – which was hardly darker than midday – the Sending came in the shape of a ghostly little girl. Out of the snow-silent night, silently, through the house-wall it came, and drifted across the room to where Thord sat.

The little girl spoke. 'I bring you a message from Kveldulf, Thord Kitten. You will be asked just three more times to tell his story. If you refuse to the last, I will kill you. This is the first time of asking. Will you – ?'

'I will never praise Kveldulf Witch!' Thord shouted, and the little girl vanished utterly. Her voice remained, saying, in every space of the house, 'Twice more will I ask, and twice more only.'

Thord laid himself down as if to sleep, but he hardly slept. He spent all that long, lonely day with hope, and fear, and one thought, that soon he might have to find out what it was like to die.

As the next midnight came near, Thord was waiting again. Silently and suddenly came the Sending, in its woman-shape. The fire turned blue and burned cold. 'Think well before you answer, Thord Kitten, because I shall ask only once more. Will you tell the story of Kveldulf's life?'

'No,' said Thord sadly. 'I never shall.'

'Tomorrow I shall come horned,' said the ghost-woman; and vanished.

Thord sat quietly on the edge of the fire-trench, and said, 'Freya, protect me, or this will be my last night alive. I wish I had spoken to my brothers when they left.'

Old Bergthora came and sat beside him. She put her hand on his knee and said, 'If I save you from the Sending, what will you do for me in return?'

'How can you save me from it? No one can.'

'Cat, Cat, I'm older than you are,' said the old woman. 'I know a lot more. I know how Kveldulf made this Sending, and I can tell you how to overcome it.'

Thord looked at her.

'Do you want to know how a witch makes a Sending?' she asked. 'First, souls must be caught, so soul-traps are hung in trees at night, when the souls of people and animals just dead are flying in the dark. They are lonely, the poor souls, and love warmth and music, so the witch makes a fire, and sings. That's what Kveldulf did. The souls flew to his fire and his singing, and were caught in his traps. But souls can't do anyone any harm. They must be given a body before they can hurt anyone. So the witch puts the souls into a body, a dead body. If enough souls are put into a corpse, the corpse can be made to move and obey the witch's orders. That is what a Sending is – a dead body stuffed with ghosts.'

'Freya guard us!' Thord said.

'She may guard us,' said Bergthora, 'but it's Odin's power that Kveldulf used to make his Sending. It is Odin's monster. Do you want to know what souls Kveldulf used? The soul of a bear, to make his

Sending strong; the soul of an eagle, so it can fly; and the souls of a woman, a man, and a little girl. And do you want to know what dead body he put them into? The body of a bull, which he skinned first, to make it more alarming.'

'And – do you know how it can be beaten?' Thord whispered.

'Odin's power and Kveldulf's spells created it,' Bergthora said. 'Odin's power and Kveldulf's spells move it. To overcome it, you must use Freya's power and your own spells.'

'I'm a farmer – a story-teller – not a witch!' Thord said. 'I know nothing about spells.'

'Cat, Cat,' said Bergthora. 'Tell me, what are Kveldulf's spells?'

Thord could not think, but he tried to answer. 'They are . . . Spells are . . . Well, words. They are words that – '

'Words!' said Bergthora. 'Yes! Spells are words, nothing more! Words chosen carefully and put together in a way that makes them strong. What else do you do when you tell a story, my Cat, but choose your words carefully and make them strong? Words are the only weapon you can use against the Sending, and Freya will surely lend you Her power. Kveldulf speaks spells for Odin, but you will speak spells for Freya, and if you are more skilful in your magic than Kveldulf is in his, you will win.'

'If I do, I will give you anything I'm able to give you in return for your help,' Thord said. 'I swear it by Freya.'

'I want you,' said the old woman.

'A ewe?' said Thord. 'I would give you a whole flock if I could.'

'No, no – *you*, Thord, *you*. You are so small and neat, I loved you as soon as I saw you. If we survive this coming night, you must marry me. You have sworn that you will, by Freya.'

Thord Cat was more speechless than any cat. The woman was so old: old and balding; old and bony; old enough to be his grandmother. But he had sworn by Freya to give her whatever she asked.

'I'll tell you the truth, Bergthora,' he said. 'I think you are too old for me, and you are not the kind of wife I ever thought I would have. But I would marry a *man* five times as old if he could tell me how to escape the Sending. I would marry a troll if that were the bargain!'

Bergthora smiled, and then spoke learnedly of spells. She gave Thord Cat good advice that day.

That night, Kveldulf Witch sent out the Sending for the last time. He said to it, 'If Thord Kitten refuses tonight, Sending, return to me with his dead body on your horns.'

The Sending flew to Thrainsstead.

It came through the wall of the house with its skin dragging and scratching behind it.

Thord had all the lamps lit, and a long-fire burning from end to end of the fire-trench, and he saw the Sending clearly. He saw its raw flesh and its blue veins laid bare. He saw its shining, goggling eyes.

'Have courage now and speak up to it, Thord,' whispered old Bergthora.

The Sending came up to Thord, and its long horns were on either side of his head, and its eyes, big as eggs, stared into his face.

'This is the last time of asking, Thord Kitten. Will you tell Kveldulf's story?' it asked.

'Don't let's talk about that again,' said Thord. 'I'm tired of it. Let's talk about the summer! I look forward to the sunshine again, don't you Sending? And the fair will be held then! Has any part of you ever been to the fair, Sending? I go every year, with my brothers.'

'Unless you answer, "yes," you won't be going this year,' said the Sending, giving him a cold and frightening look from its bulging eyes.

The look made Thord shiver, but he would not be stopped from chattering. 'Last year, when I was at the fair,' he said, 'I saw a little girl, lost. She didn't know she was lost, because she was so busy looking at everything there was for sale . . .' And Thord told of how the ships come to Iceland from Norway and Scotland, Ireland and England, with beautiful wood, with stone pots and brilliant blue and scarlet cloth, with shining gold and tin; of how ships brought salt blocks, and green stone, and red copper, from Denmark and Sweden and the land of the Rus; and all they brought was laid out for sale at the fair.

Thord's hands and eyes told of the fair, as well as his mouth, and as the Sending listened, it fidgeted. It wagged its horned head. It rolled its unclosing eyes. It clattered its hooves. It was as if Thord's words and gestures made it itch.

Thord's words and movements were disturbing the human spirits inside the Sending. The spirits had been to fairs when they had been alive. They remembered the bright spreads of coloured cloths, and the expression on Thord's face as he told of them made the spirits feel all the pleasure of sunlight and colour. The movements of his hands and head as he told of the crowded fairground made the spirits feel again all the sway and noise and jostle of so many people, all enjoying life together in the one place. The spirits listened and watched intently; and the Sending did not like the way this made it feel.

'Then the little girl looked round and saw nobody she knew,' said Thord, 'so she started to cry. I picked her up and said, "Why are you pulling such faces?" And I pulled faces at *her*. My brother Haki bought her a cake, and she was soon laughing.'

The Sending shook its head and snorted. One spirit in particular was listening and watching so hard that the Sending's eyes and ears tingled.

'Haki put her up on his shoulders because he's much taller than me, and we walked about the fair,' said Thord. 'She could see the tops of everyone's heads up there on Haki's shoulders, and everyone could see her, swaying about as if she was on top of a ship's mast. We walked twice round the fair and then her mother spotted her and came to get her. Her mother and father were traders from England. They gave Haki and me each an English knife for finding her – here's my knife, look. They make good knives in England. We were close friends with that English family when the fair ended. We said, "When you come back to Iceland again, you must come and stay with us at Thrainsstead." They came again the very next year, but it was a sad meeting.'

Thord stopped there and shook his head sadly. The Sending did not mean to say anything, but the spirits inside it were at work, and the Sending's mouth popped open to ask, 'Why?'

'The little girl was dead,' said Thord.

There was so much shock and interest among the human spirits inside the Sending that it felt ill.

'A witch stole away her soul, and so she died,' Thord said.

The Sending felt the oddest sensation of all, then. A part of itself went numb. Not a leg or an ear, but a part of its thinking stopped; numb.

'What about Kveldulf's story, story-teller?' the Sending demanded. 'Will you tell it? Answer!'

'I once knew a story-teller,' Thord said. 'She kept a farm. She was a wonderful story-teller. I used to go and see her, and the thing about her was: she loved her farm, loved every crumb of soil and every blade of grass on it. She used to ride about it, to keep an eye on everything. There wasn't a single sheep sick or a single seed sprouting that she didn't know about. People used to go to her for advice – my brothers did – because she was such a good farmer. And then her daughter, who had married a man a long way off, fell sick, and Hild left her farm to go and see what she could do for her. She was away for months. Every time her daughter seemed better, Hild would think she could go home, and then her daughter would be worse again and she would have to stay.

'Hild missed her farm. Oh, people brought her news of it, but she could never be sure they were telling her everything. She wanted to see it for herself. Anyway, at last her daughter got well again, and Hild started home. She set out at a gallop. There was a hill, and she knew that when she reached the top of that hill, she would see her farm below her. So she rode for the hill. But – '

Again Thord stopped, and shook his head.

I don't care about this woman, the Sending thought. But the human spirits inside it did, and the Sending had to ask, 'But – what?'

'She never got there,' said Thord. 'A witch was out, fishing for souls – and he caught Hild's soul. She never saw her farm again. And now it's owned by a man who's ruining it.'

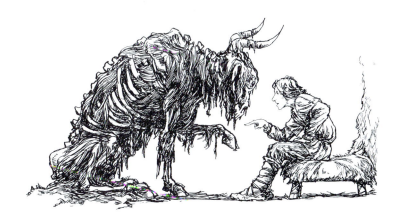

The Sending had a feeling that something was boiling and bubbling in its chest. And again it had that peculiar feeling that part of its thinking had gone numb.

'No more stories, Thord Kitten, no more! An answer from you is all that I want!' said the Sending.

'I knew a man once who hated stories,' said Thord.

The Sending put its bull-face into his. 'No – more – stories!' But the spirits inside it wanted to hear stories. Many people would happily listen to stories until the end of time, whether they were alive or dead.

'Only a short story,' Thord said. 'He couldn't stand stories, this man. His name was Thorgeir. "What is the point of stories?" he would say. "They keep you from your work, and when you hear the end, it's never worth waiting for. It's always just as you guessed it would be."'

'Exactly how I feel about them,' the Sending said.

'So he would never listen to stories, not even if Hild was telling them. He would go to some other part of the house and do something useful.'

The Sending could feel the spirits inside it still listening, and it said, 'A sensible man, this Thorgeir!'

'Maybe he was sensible not to listen to stories,' said Thord, 'but it was the end of him, just the same.'

And then he shut his mouth and seemed as if he would never speak again. He poked the fire.

The Sending stamped. 'Why? How was it the end of him?'

'Because – one night – ,' Thord said.

'Yes?' cried the Sending. 'One night! What?'

'One night he heard a voice in the darkness outside his house – a voice calling his name.'

The Sending felt the spirits inside it shiver.

'And – he went outside to see who it was!' Thord said.

'And who was it?' breathed the Sending.

'A witch! And the witch stole his soul, and he died. If he had listened to stories, he would have known that you should never go outside when you hear your name called at night.'

The Sending leapt up and trampled about the

house in a temper, shouting, 'Stories are all tricks and snares for fools' ears! That ending was not worth waiting for – why did I wait for it?'

In the middle of its rage, it felt another numbness.

Now the human spirits inside it began to call out for themselves.

'Tell us another, Cat!'

'There's a bear in here with us – tell one about a bear!'

'Tell one for an eagle!'

And Thord Cat, who loved to tell stories, and would tell them even to spirits and monsters if they asked him, immediately began to tell a tale about a bear whose soul was stolen by a witch; and when that was ended, he told about an eagle whose soul was stolen by a witch.

Though the stories had the same ending, the listening spirits did not think them boring. Neither the eagle nor the bear had ever guessed that a man could know so much about them, and they listened with fascination as Thord told them of the lives they had once led. Then, from the tone of his voice, and the expression on his face, they knew that danger was entering the story – was it the witch? And would the eagle – or the bear – escape? They guessed that neither would, but the half-hope that they might, made them listen all the harder. And when, in the end, the witch stole the souls and killed the animals, how the spirits were filled with anger and sorrow! This turmoil of the spirits inside it made the Sending feel so ill, it had to lie down.

'Now a story for the bull,' said the spirits, and Thord gladly began to tell the story of a fine young bull-calf – one who had been owned by a witch.

Everyone is interested most by talk of themselves. The bull listened keenly to the story. It thought to itself: if he says anything about bulls that I don't like, I shall stamp on him.

Thord told of the life the young bull-calf had led in the mountain-fields during the spring and summer; and of the long winters it had spent shut in a dark byre. Everything Thord spoke of, the bull had done, or thought, or felt; and as the bull listened, it thought again and again: that is true; that is so; that is just what it is like! And the bull was astonished that this little creature, so small and weak and so like a man, could know so much of its bullish life.

The bull thought, 'He looks like a man, but he must really be a strange and oddly shaped little bull.' And it thought, 'Kveldulf Witch has sent me to kill one of my own kind!'

'But this bull had hardly grown to its full size,' said Thord, 'and had all its life yet to sample, when Kveldulf Witch came with an axe and killed it. And then the witch did worse. He made its dead body a bee-hive buzzing with stranger-spirits, and forced it to a heavy death-life. It had to do all that Kveldulf ordered it to do – and he made it do such things that it was hated.'

The bull quivered with anger and astonishment. The terrible thing that Kveldulf had done to it had never been made clear in its mind before.

'Why, why did he take my life away? I am made a monster. I am unloved. I want to be alive again, on my hillside!' A pool of tears formed round the bull's huge body. 'But I am dead,' the monster sobbed, 'and the dead can never live again as they once did.'

Bergthora took Thord's arm. She had a surprisingly strong grip for an old woman. 'Those were good stories, Cat,' she said, 'but you have not yet answered the question. Will you tell Kveldulf's story?'

Thord was dismayed. If he answered, the Sending would kill him. Did Bergthora want him killed?

Bergthora spoke sternly, a very grand beggar-woman suddenly. 'Answer, Thord Cat! Will you praise Kveldulf, or will you not?'

'No,' Thord said. 'I won't and I never will.'

'Then come Sending, do your work!' Bergthora cried. 'Slice him! Pierce him! Carry him to Kveldulf on your horns!'

The Sending roared and leapt – but not at Thord. It leapt along inside the house; it rampaged between the walls in a fury; it danced with rage in the fire-trench, all among the flames, showering sparks. From it came the roaring of a bear, the screaming of an eagle and the screeching of a woman, the angry shouting of human voices. The Sending rushed about with such force, there seemed nowhere for Bergthora and Thord to be safe.

'Do you hear it?' Bergthora asked. 'The spirits are angry against Kveldulf and full of pity for you. That is what your story-telling has done! All the spirits in the Sending wish you to live, and they are fighting against the power of Odin and Kveldulf! Be with us now, Freya! Thord – the Sending is yours now! Speak to it quickly! Send it against Kveldulf while your power lasts!'

Thord yelled and yelled, 'In the name of Freya, go to Kveldulf! Go!'

Straight up and through the turf-roof flew the Sending, flying on the spirit of an eagle. Back through the darkness to Kveldulf it flew, with vengeance in its thoughts. People at distant farms heard the din of its rage as it flew, and Haki and Grimm heard it in the house where they were staying.

When the sound of the Sending's passing had faded, Haki said to Grimm, 'Now we had better go home and bury Thord's body.'

So they made a slow, cold and unhappy journey back through the snow to Thrainsstead. They stood looking at the house a while before crossing the yard and opening the door. They did not want to go in because they were sure they would find Thord's dead body, and probably Bergthora's too.

Their amazement, their joy and their relief when they found Thord and Bergthora sitting side by side on the edge of the fire-trench, eating porridge! Haki and Grimm hid Thord from sight with their hugs, and they hugged Bergthora too; and they asked a dozen times to be told the story of how they had escaped the Sending. 'Not until you have seen us married!' said Thord.

His brothers were puzzled. Who was he to marry?

'Bergthora!' said Thord. 'You must be the witnesses.' And he ran to fetch Thor's Hammer from its place on the wall behind the guest-chair.

'Cat, is this a joke?' asked Haki. 'If it is, it's a bad one.'

'Bergthora's advice saved me from the Sending,' said Thord, 'and in return, I swore by Freya I would marry her. So – hear our vows!'

And he raised the Hammer, to begin the wedding vows. Haki seized his arm.

'Thord! Think how people will laugh to see you married to a toothless woman old as your grandmother! No one knows of this promise but us, and we will think no worse of you for breaking it.'

Bergthora said nothing, but watched Thord Cat with sharp eyes.

Thord gave Haki an angry look and shook his hand from his arm. He raised the Hammer, and said, 'I, Thord Thrainsson, swear in the presence of Thor, and before those here present, that from this day forward I take Bergthora as my legal wife.' He put the Hammer into Bergthora's lap.

Bergthora stood, the Hammer in her hands. Her legs straightened, as straight as Thord's. Her spine was straight. Back went her shoulders, up went her head on a long, strong neck. This ancient, bent old woman was standing as upright as a girl!

Bergthora's hair became so plentiful and heavy that it pulled out its own hair-pins and fell down around her, no longer thin and scanty rat-tails, but glistening, thick, weighty dark hanks.

And Bergthora's face changed. Her wrinkled, folded skin became tight and smooth; her eyes became large and dark. In the place of ancient Bergthora, there stood beside Thord a strong, beautiful young woman, with brooches of gold at her shoulders, a golden ring round her throat, and a sword at her side.

The silence of the house tingled with astonishment and fear. Haki and Grimm could not but remember times when they had spoken sharply to this witch they had taken for an old beggar-woman, and Haki remembered how he had urged Thord to break his promise to her.

Thord Cat was so astounded that his legs shook
and he sank to his knees. 'Oh Freya defend me!' he
said. 'I have married Freya!' For he thought the
young woman so imposing and beautiful that she
must be the god Freya, who had disguised Herself as
Bergthora.

But the young woman looked down on him,
smiled, and shook her head. She raised the
Hammer, and said, 'I, Marya Marevna, Ruler and
Defender of Ultima Thule by grace of Freya, swear
in the presence of Thor and before those here
present, that from this day forward I take Thord to
be my legal spouse.'

And Haki and Grimm whispered to one another,
'The Queen of Ultima Thule!'

Said Marya Marevna, 'I am a witch, a warrior
and a Queen, and I make no ordinary marriage. I
called to Freya for help, and threw the rune-stones
in Her name. The stones fell and spelled out, *Thord*

*Cat.* I asked where this cat was to be found, and the stones told me where. So here I came, in magical disguise, to find Thord Cat and to discover for myself his looks and character.'

She turned to Thord, and said to him, 'Your face and figure I liked at first sight, but if you had not given me sympathy when you thought me an old beggar-woman, I would have considered you worth nothing. If you had praised Kveldulf Witch, or ever given in to his threats, I would have left you in disgust. If your skill with words had not been great enough to overcome the Sending, I would have let it kill you. And if you had not kept your promise to marry me, I would have struck you dead myself. But, Thord Cat, you are beautiful, kind, brave, honest, and a fine story-teller. If you will be my husband, you shall come with me to Ultima Thule as a prince, and be my court's story-teller. But if this is not what you wish, I know you will tell me so honestly, and we shall break our marriage now, and go our own way.'

Thord thought of the storms and sunlit ice of Ultima Thule, at the top and edge of the world. He thought of the foreign kings and far-travelled merchants he would meet there, all with their own stories to tell. And he looked at the Queen, who was as beautiful as Freya. He held out his hand to her and said, 'Let's stay married until we tire of each other. That will be time enough to part.'

The Queen took his hand, and was about to speak when frightening bellows and stampings came from the yard outside the house. Haki went to the door, looked out, and came back saying, 'The Sending!'

'There is nothing to fear,' said the Queen. She took Thord's hand and, together, they went out into the yard.

There, in the darkness of the winter's day, stood the Sending in its bull-shape, steaming at the nostrils, its skinless sides heaving, lights glowing on its horns.

But over its back lay the body of Kveldulf Witch. The Sending had taken its revenge, and Odin had been paid His life.

All the spirits in the bull's body cried out, 'Thord Cat, set us free! We are tied together in this carcase with no home and no help. All people fear us and none will give us a kind look – loose us, loose us!'

Thord spread his hands in distress, for he had no idea how to give the creature the help it asked.

'He has his spells, but he is no witch,' said the Queen. 'I shall release you. I shall untangle the spirits that make you, and give them all rest. Bring me a handful of oatmeal.'

She held out her hand – and Thord ran to an outhouse where meal was stored, and brought her back the handful of meal. She made him hold it out at arm's length, and she blew into his hand, and blew a puff of the meal away. As the oatmeal flew in the wind, the soul of the little girl was released from the bull and flew in the wind to its proper place. The Queen blew away all the oatmeal, and with it she blew away the souls of the woman, the bear, the eagle and the man. When Thord's hand was empty, the bull's body lay dead in the yard, with the body of Kveldulf beneath it.

'The Sending need no more be feared,' said the Queen, 'but Kveldulf Witch is another matter. He had an angry, wicked soul, and I think he will not rest quiet in any grave, but will come out and visit your house by night.'

Haki and Grimm had come out into the yard, and they were alarmed to hear this. They begged her to tell them how to protect themselves against Kveldulf's ghost.

The Queen said, 'When you bury Kveldulf, you must drive a good, thick, long wooden stake through his heart, deep into the earth beneath him, to pin him in his grave. Put a large boulder on top, to make it hard for him to come out. But best of all, on top of him, bury this bull he mistreated so badly. The bull hates Kveldulf now, and it will guard him for you, and prevent him doing harm.'

All that she advised was done.

In a pasture below Thrainsstead the brothers hacked a grave from the earth, and laid Kveldulf in it. Grimm hammered a stake through his heart, and the bull was dragged into place on top of the witch. Finally, with ropes and horses, a boulder was set above the grave.

But to tell of happier things: the Thrainssons and the Queen passed the winter cheerfully together, and were not bothered by Kveldulf during the day or the night.

Spring came, and it was time for Thord to go with his wife to his new home. Haki and Grimm rode with them to the coast, to see the last of their brother. At the sea's edge, the Queen took from her pocket a tiny ship, no longer than her hand. Gently, she put it on the surface of the sea, and it grew and became a large, fast ship, complete with crew. The Queen set the crew to emptying the ship's hold of gold, silver and precious stones. 'These, I think,' said the Queen to Haki and Grimm, 'will buy you sheep to replace those the Sending killed.'

Then the Queen and Thord went on board the ship and sailed out of sight over the cold sea, leaving Haki and Grimm rich but sad, wondering when they would ever see their youngest brother again.

But every year the Queen sent her ship from Ultima Thule, to bring Haki and Grimm to her court, where Thord was longing to see them. And when Haki and Grimm married, their wives and children went with them, and were entertained like the children of kings.

Year after year they sailed to Ultima Thule, for the Queen never grew tired of Thord, nor he of her. With the favour of Freya, they were happy and had five daughters and five sons, every one of them a story-teller and a witch.

All this happened so long ago that now no one knows where the land of Ultima Thule was or is, and for all we know Marya Marevna still rules there, at the top and edge of the world, with Thord Cat to tell her stories.

It happened so long ago that no one knows where the farm of Thrainsstead stood: so no one knows where Kveldulf Witch lies buried with the bull on top of him.

But wherever the grave is, let's hope that Kveldulf – and the skinned bull – are still in it.